BOUNDLESS

BOUNDLESS

DRAGON APPROVED™ BOOK THIRTEEN

RAMY VANCE

MICHAEL ANDERLE

DISRUPTIVE IMAGINATION

THE BOUNDLESS TEAM

Thanks to the JIT Readers

Jeff Goode
Rachel Beckford
Deb Mader
Kerry Mortimer
Dorothy Lloyd
Veronica Stephan-Miller
Kelly O'Donnell
Diane L. Smith

If we've missed anyone, please let us know!

Editor
The Skyhunter Editing Team

Copyright © 2020 by LMBPN Publishing
Cover Art by Jake @ J Caleb Design
http://jcalebdesign.com / jcalebdesign@gmail.com
Cover copyright © LMBPN Publishing
A Michael Anderle Production

LMBPN Publishing
PMB 196, 2540 South Maryland Pkwy
Las Vegas, NV 89109

First US Edition, June 2020
eBook ISBN: 978-1-64202-978-9
Print ISBN: 978-1-64202-979-6

DEDICATION

To Dragons in Space...I know they're not a person, but hot-damn! As a concept it is intoxicating!

—Ramy

To Family, Friends and Those Who Love to Read. May We All Enjoy Grace to Live the Life We Are Called.

— Michael

CHAPTER ONE

Vardis stood in the doorway of Alex's hospital room. He didn't say anything, but his eyes betrayed his purpose. The alien was seething with energy. It was like looking at a lightbulb exceeding its wattage. He seemed unable to contain himself.

Alex had only just pulled herself out of Vardis' mental labyrinth. She still wasn't sure what was real. Her memories seemed tacked on, or like they could have been changed without her even realizing it. The only thing she was certain of was that she was in the real world now.

Roy was still having trouble adjusting to being outside the mental plane. He didn't look as sick as he had while navigating through Vardis' and Alex's memories, but he didn't look like he was up for a fight.

Vardis took a slow, deliberate step into the room as if he were savoring the confusion he had caused to both Alex and Roy. He was gloating.

Alex wasn't going to take the bait. "What are you doing here?"

Vardis looked around the room, energy still pouring from

his body. "I came to see if you were okay. I heard about the explosion and wanted to check on your health."

Alex knew that was a lie. Even though she didn't have any proof, she knew the explosion that had put her in the med-bay was caused by Vardis. She didn't need proof that Vardis was trying to hurt her, though. Roy had been involved in the psychic attack as well. He'd back her up. "I'm onto you," Alex threatened.

Vardis closed the door behind him as he walked farther in the room. He looked from Alex to Roy, watching them both closely. "I do not know what you're talking about," he murmured, feigning ignorance. The smug tone in his voice was obvious. "They're going to be transporting the shard in a little while. I thought you should know."

"You can't use that weapon!"

A pulse went through the room, a subtle ripple as if someone had lightly pressed their fingertip to water. Alex looked at Roy to see if he felt the distortion as well, but she found herself moving extremely slowly as if she were trying to move through gelatin.

Then she heard Vardis' voice in her head, lacking the prior smugness but sounding nearly frantic, almost mad. "We need to use the weapon as soon as possible," he said. "It is time for this war to end, for the Dark One to pay for every-thing he's put us through."

For the first time since she'd started suspecting Vardis, Alex realized the alien might not be of sound mind, and it seemed like he was quickly unraveling. "If we use that weapon, it's going to destroy everything we know. It'll destroy what we are fighting for."

"Not what *you're* fighting for. Don't you understand anything about dimensions and universes, human? It's powerful enough to destroy a universe. Middang3ard isn't your home, this is. Once the weapon is used on Middang3ard, the other eight surviving realms will keep on living. They'll be able to experience life free of the Dark One."

Alex hadn't realized the distinction until just now. Middang3ard wasn't Earth, nor were the elvish or gnomish realms. They were all layered over each other like a pile of crepes. Vardis was only talking about discarding one of the crepes.

Would that be so bad? Middang3ard was just a hub of different species, most of them working on the war effort. They could be evacuated; there was no reason they had to die. And the rest of the realm...

Alex couldn't believe she was even thinking about the option. It was practically genocide, and not worth it. The thought of losing any number of lives to destroy the Dark One made Alex's stomach turn.

"Is it any different than the lives Myrddin sacrifices to fight the Dark One?"

Vardis' voice broke Alex away from her thoughts. Now she wasn't certain if the initial thought she'd had about letting Middang3ard be destroyed had originated from her or the alien.

It had been the same when she'd spoken to the Dark One. Even though Alex's telepathy was getting stronger at a rapid rate, she wasn't sure if it was on par with either the Dark One's or Vardis'. Maybe they were strong enough to influence her mind in ways she didn't even know about.

Alex shook away the alien's words. "No, they're different. We'd all be dead if Myrddin hadn't organized everything."

"Yet there have been sacrifices. Your arm, for instance. There are things we lose that we never get back. That's all this is, a sacrifice. The immensity of that sacrifice is as large as that which we hope to remove."

Something about Vardis' voice had changed. It had lost its manic tone and was low and almost comforting, a distortion he did not seem to be aware of. Alex would have assumed it was an entirely different person.

"Myrddin asked me to fight. It wasn't something I was forced into. It was my decision. What you're planning is monstrous."

Vardis raised his hand, his palm facing Roy. "No, monstrous would be focusing on your friend's brain long enough to reduce it to a gray puddle on the floor. That would be senseless, unnecessary, and monstrous, to do that just to see your pain. What I'm proposing is that you and I, that *we* save the realms together. Keep quiet, and we can all live through this."

Alex pushed back telepathically, warding off Vardis' influence. "I'm not going to kill millions of people."

"Just like the Dark One asked you, right?"

Alex's heart dropped. She wasn't sure how Vardis knew about the conversation she'd had with the Dark One. Or maybe he didn't. He could have been bluffing. It wouldn't have been hard to deduce that the Dark One had reached out to Alex during the battle. "He didn't ask me anything," Alex answered.

Vardis was silent for a second, watching Alex as if he were trying to discern the truth of her words.

The uncertainty in his eyes was extremely comforting to her. If he could be confused, he didn't have full access to her mind. She felt uncertainty coming off him.

That must have been how it worked. They could pick up on each other's feelings, and things that could be given away with body language seemed to amplify the thoughts of the individual. If Alex could keep her body language in control, it would be harder for Vardis to read her.

Vardis, on the other hand, didn't get himself under control. His emotions were as palpable as the psychic energy coming off his body.

Alex decided to push the alien. "That's the difference between you and me. You're willing to sacrifice everyone around you, and yet you don't fight. Sounds a little cowardly to me."

Anger filled the room as Vardis ground his teeth. "I have sacrificed more than you will ever understand. All of us sacrificed so much."

The alien's eyes went glossy for a second, the bright white energy fading before he looked around the room as if he had just been transported into it.

The energy came back and he screamed in rage. "All of them died! Do you understand? *Every one of them!*"

A psychic blast tore through the room as time returned to normal.

Alex and Roy were flung against the wall and hit hard enough to crack the concrete.

The sudden time dilation had caught Alex off-guard, but the blast was weak compared to what she'd gone through in Vardis' mind. He must have been distracted. Whatever was going on in his head was a weakness, one Alex wanted to exploit. "Where were you when they died? It didn't seem like you could do anything to help them."

When Vardis spoke, it was in a voice Alex had never heard him use. It was high-pitched and more frenzied than before, his voice cracking with every other word. "I did everything I could! None of them believed me! None of them were willing to do what needed to be done! That's why they are no more. But we continue. We will not let the Dark One win."

Who is the "we" Vardis keeps talking about? Alex thought. *He's never done that before. This guy must be crazier than I thought.*

Roy was getting to his feet, shaken by what had happened.

He still managed to draw his pistol faster than Alex could see and fire.

One of the shots hit Vardis in the arm, flinging him back. The alien didn't seem hurt, though. He raised his hand, and Roy went flying.

Alex reached out and tried to telekinetically pull Roy back down to the ground as he writhed in pain. "So, that's the plan? You couldn't do anything to keep your people alive? The best plan you got is to wipe out an entire universe? I wouldn't be surprised if you were the one who wiped out your people."

Roy fell to the ground as Vardis took a step back. "*What did you just say?*"

"You heard me. You keep going on about how the Dark One killed your people, but we were in your mind too. I didn't see one memory of the Dark One. Just you and a bunch of dead people like you."

The walls in the room started to shake and the glass in the windows vibrated. "How dare you!" Vardis growled.

The door opened and a nurse walked into the room. She froze when she saw the standoff between Vardis and Alex. "I could come back later," she murmured and let herself out.

Before the door could close, it exploded like a grenade had just gone off, slicing the nurse's face and leaving her a bloody mess on the floor.

Alex screamed in rage, seeing how casually Vardis had treated a human life, and drew her scythe, rushing at Vardis while pulling him closer with her telekinesis.

Vardis pushed back as hard as he could, stopping Alex for a second as he ran.

It wasn't in Alex's head. Vardis was stronger in real life than in the psychic plane. It must have been because his attention wasn't split. Her powers didn't feel like they were anywhere close to his.

Roy was back on his feet. He ran over to the nurse who had been attacked and held her head up. She coughed up blood, and there were tears in her eyes as she looked about fearfully. "Where does it hurt?" Roy asked.

The nurse looked down at her stomach and pulled up her shirt. There were cuts all over her torso as well as her face. "They're superficial," she managed, her voice eerily professional. "I'll survive."

"We'll get help."

Roy looked at Alex. "We can't let him get too far away. Come on."

Alex followed Roy as he commed for a medical team to come to Alex's room. They raced after Vardis, and Alex wondered what other tricks the alien had up his sleeve.

CHAPTER TWO

R oy patched himself into the base's cameras as he and Alex pursued Vardis to see if he could find the alien and figure out where he was heading to. "Found him! He's going for the hangar. We can cut him off before he gets there. Follow me."

Roy turned a corner a moment later and stopped. He pointed at an air duct. "You're not claustrophobic, are you?"

Alex looked dubiously at the air duct. "I prefer the open sky, but I'm not going to have a panic attack or anything. Why do we have to use the ducts, though?"

"It's a straight shot to the hangar. We'll beat him to the punch and be able to take him out faster."

Roy pulled the grate off the air duct and knelt to give Alex a boost. She climbed up to it and slid in. It wasn't as tight as she'd thought it was going to be. Roy pulled himself up behind her and directed her forward.

Alex crawled through the duct, already anxious to get out, but she followed Roy's instructions and turned where he told her to. It wasn't long before he told her to stop. "Right below us," he said. "Go ahead and get out."

Alex punched out the grate with her bionic arm and leaped out of the duct.

The hangar was empty of any personnel but filled with a variety of transportation options: decommissioned fighter jets, some tanks, and a small collection of helicopters. There were exo-suits lined up against the wall that didn't look like they'd ever been used. Alex remembered reading about them and how there were some groups in Myrddin's army that were composed of soldiers without magic who only used that kind of suit.

The lights in the hangar flickered on, and Alex saw how vast it was. Her initial impression of what the hangar held had been very misguided. There was nearly triple the amount of military junk than she'd originally thought. "Okay, what's the plan?" Alex asked.

Roy walked around, peeking behind a helicopter. "I think we beat him here, so it's an ambush. Don't know why he's heading to the hangar, though."

Roy checked his visor's feed of Vardis running through the hallways. "Yeah, he's still heading this way, but it looks like he's doing something. Messing with the cameras or something. It's hard to see through the feed."

Vardis looked directly into the camera and Roy's feed disappeared. "Guess that sums that one up. He's knocking out the cameras."

"Maybe he's trying to make sure we don't call backup."

Roy shook his head as he walked back over to Alex. "Doesn't make any sense. If we were going to call for backup, we already would have."

"Uh, just asking, how come we haven't called for backup?"

Roy was pacing and scratching the back of his head. "Vardis was smart. When we were bringing you back, a couple of other explosions went off in the base as well. We evacuated most of it. This place isn't built for an attack.

None of the dragons had been outfitted. And we still didn't know the nature of the attack. Perfect time for Vardis to take out one person and not get caught."

Alex blushed and met Roy's eyes. "He didn't start by trying to attack me. For a bit, everything froze, and he tried to convince me to help him set off the weapon on Middang3ard."

Roy leaned against one of the helicopters as he watched the door of the hangar. "Why do you look so bummed out? Did you agree? Is this a big double-cross?"

Alex threw her hands up, worried until she saw Roy smiling. "No. I'd never do that, but it felt like he had some good points. Some very good points."

"Let me guess. People must make sacrifices. Myrddin sacrifices people all the time. What's the difference between what he wants to do and what Myrddin has done?"

Alex was surprised Roy hit the nail on the head. "How did you know he said that?"

"Because I've come across my share of megalomaniacal psychos before. You think they'd come up with something more original by now, but nope. Everyone basically says the same thing. Sounds good the first time, but after your third psycho, it seems like they all get the same script. I'm waiting for a bad guy with a little more creativity to show up. Even the Dark One, who wants to enslave all of reality for no reason. Guy doesn't even have a tragic backstory."

Alex chuckled as she thought of what might be motivating the Dark One. "You know, I never thought of that. Guess he *is* pretty bland."

"All I'm saying is that these guys all say the same crap, and you don't have to feel bad because it sounds right. The best lies have a little bit of truth in them. But you're solid, Alex. I know that. We all do. We trust you. You don't have to be worried that we'll doubt you just because you have a secret conversation. Not going to happen."

"That means a lot to me. It really does."

Roy lit his cigar and puffed out a heavy cloud of smoke. "The Dark One. Even the name is…meh. Trust me, all these psychos are the same."

The hangar's double doors opened. Vardis walked into the hangar, looking around as if he were suspecting an ambush.

Roy's idea of an ambush must have been a loose interpretation of the word because he hadn't bothered trying to hide or come up with a plan for when Vardis arrived. "Ambush" meant "surprise," from what it looked like.

For a moment, Vardis didn't seem to notice Roy and Alex. Maybe there was enough crap in the room that Vardis couldn't see them. Even though the lights were on, it wasn't particularly bright.

Vardis floated through the air. At first, Alex thought it was to look for her and Roy, but the alien wasn't searching for anything on the ground. Instead, he found the security cameras up in the corners of the hangar and ripped them off, then crushed the cameras to bits and flung the pieces to the ground.

"Why the hell is he getting rid of all the cameras?" Roy muttered.

Alex had been wondering the same thing. The only obvious answer was that he didn't want anyone to know what he was up to, but that was a convoluted, ass-backward way to keep anyone from knowing he'd gone rogue. He could have just waited to attack when they had all gotten back to Middang3ard. "I have no idea what he's up to, so what's the plan?"

"Plan? Oh, I was going to attack him. Take him dead or alive. Dead, probably. He seems like a fighter."

"I meant, do you have a plan for how to do that?"

"With my guns. Not a joke. I mean my actual guns."

Alex sighed as she shook her head. "So, guns blazing?"

"I figure you will use whatever the hell kinda powers you have now, and we'll whittle him down. Shouldn't take too long. We saw how strong he was on the moon. We can take him."

Alex had all but forgotten about Vardis' display of power on the moon. It seemed like a very long time ago. Roy was right, though. Alex was a competent fighter, and Roy had decades of years of experience. Maybe even more if the memories that they'd shared were any indication of his age.

Alex was preparing to say something when she noticed Roy staring longingly at one of the exo-suits. "You don't see the 850 series anymore," he explained. "They were faster and stronger than anything else we've put out."

"How come you don't use them, then?"

"Neural connection is a little bit off. Fried a couple of brains. But it's not every day you get to take one for a spin. You get started with fly-boy up there. I've got an idea."

"An idea or a plan?"

Roy turned and jogged backward, shrugging. "Is there a difference?" He took off toward the exo-suit.

Alex concentrated and lifted herself into the air. She couldn't fly like Vardis did, but she was able to lift herself, nearly doubling her jump range. It was a lot harder than Vardis made it look. "Vardis!" Alex shouted.

The alien stopped in his tracks and looked around, trying to pinpoint the place from which his name had been called. While Vardis searched for Alex, the dragonrider suppressed her emotions and thoughts to make it harder for Vardis to find her.

He used his telekinesis to throw one of the fighter jets out of the way. It looked effortless, as if it had taken a fraction of his attention. He'd thrown the jet the way someone flicks a gnat off their arm. Alex could see she was nowhere near Vardis' level in the real world.

But that didn't matter. Alex hadn't been going to psychic classes for the last few months. She'd been training as a dragonrider, and a rider didn't rely on one trick to deal with a situation.

Alex pulled out her scythe and watched Vardis floating above, still trying to find her. When Vardis passed over her, Alex flung her scythe at him, guiding it with her mind.

The scythe hit Vardis in the shoulder, and the blade stuck in his skin. He screamed as he ripped the blade out of his arm and tossed it down to the ground. Then he stretched out his hands and pushed back every vehicle in front of him.

The rider dove behind a moving helicopter. It had become apparent Vardis had no idea where she was. He was flailing, but by knocking over so much crap, he had given her an unintentional advantage.

Alex slid into the helicopter closest to her and propped open its sliding door, then scanned through her inventory. There were more weapons than her scythe loaded into her dragon anchor. The scythe was the easiest for her to use, but Alex had trained with every weapon she owned.

The gravity disruption grenades would work well with an ice grenade. Alex thought about her pistol but realized she wasn't a good enough shot.

She poked her head out of the helicopter and saw Vardis floating above, still searching for her. She tossed the gravity disruption grenade on the ground and watched as it rolled toward Vardis. When it was under him, she remotely detonated it.

A small gravity well opened, pulling Vardis out of the air so quickly that he didn't have a chance to react. As he fought to get away from the well, Alex tossed the ice grenade at him and detonated it.

A blast of ice shot out and flash-froze the alien where he stood.

Alex leaped out from her cover and raced toward Vardis. On the way, she scooped up her scythe and jumped over an overturned tank. Vardis wouldn't see this coming. Even if he did, Alex knew how fast she was. She'd get there before the alien even had a chance.

She leaped over another tank, landing in front of him. The alien's eyes went wide as Alex brought her scythe down on the side of his neck. Then she pulled back her bionic arm and let loose a punch that would put a hole in a concrete wall.

The ice around Vardis began to crack and small sheets fell off. Then he flew into the hangar's wall.

Alex knew that wasn't going to be enough to take out the alien. Now that the attack had started, she wasn't going to be able to let up. She ran after him, then flung herself through the air and landed on top of him. She cupped her hands together and brought down a double fist on his chest. Even through the ice, she could see his eyes widen in pain. Then she grabbed her scythe, ready to take off Vardis' head.

The ice around the alien's body shattered as a psychic shockwave knocked Alex off the alien.

She hit the floor and skidded into a fighter jet. As she got to her feet, she could see Vardis doing the same. They glared at each other from across the hangar. This was going to be it —their last stand.

CHAPTER THREE

Vardis raised his hand to attack the dragonrider. Before he could do anything, Roy barreled into him from the side, and the alien careened into the side of a tank.

Roy was wearing the exo-suit, a tight-fitting mechanical spine that went up to the back of his neck. The exo-suit also connected to the arms, wired to the tips of Roy's fingers and extending down his legs to his ankles. "You thought you guys were going to finish without me?" He chuckled.

Alex moved to take advantage of Vardis' surprise, heading for the tank the alien had crashed into.

He was already back on his feet, and he whipped his hands in front of him, sending the tank toward Alex.

Alex punched it with her bionic hand, slowing it down but not enough to keep from being flung back.

Roy leaped to help Alex. He hit the tank with his feet and pushed hard, which launched the tank back at Vardis.

The alien dodged to the right and scampered across the floor on all fours before jumping at Alex, who had just gotten to her feet. He tackled her, and the two went rolling across the cement. Vardis raised his hand, a psychic blast forming in his palm.

Before Vardis could bring down his fist, Alex punched him in the face with her bionic arm. The force of the attack knocked him off, and he hit the ground and rolled behind the tank he'd thrown. He raised the tank and ripped it in two, then sent half the tank at Alex and the other half at Roy.

Roy managed to get out of the way, and his half smashed into a jet fighter behind him, crumpling the jet's steel skin.

Alex also dodged her half of the tank but reached out and threw it back at Vardis, who floated into the air above Alex and Roy. "Do you think that is enough to stop me? You lack conviction! If you cannot do what needs to be done, how do you think you will end this?" the alien screeched.

The manic frenzy was back in Vardis' voice. Whatever was going on in his head was getting worse. Alex waved for Roy to follow her as the alien started cackling madly. "Sounds like he's losing his mind," Alex remarked.

Roy ducked behind a tank. "Yeah, that *is* what it sounds like. I didn't think he was going to be so tough. Guess now's the time to call those reinforcements, even if it's going to take a minute." He pulled up his HUD. "Oh, crap, something's blocking communication. Must be him."

The sound of steel hitting steel broke up the conversation, and the tank the two were hiding behind pushed back against them. "I'll try to reach Chine!" Alex shouted.

Roy rolled out from behind their cover, drew both of his plasma pistols, and fired a couple of bolts at Vardis as he ducked behind another tank.

The alien waved away the plasma blasts, sending them into the wall.

Alex was tired of being on the defensive, but she didn't know what else to do. Vardis was much more powerful when he was using telekinesis. Then Alex remembered how erratically he had behaved when she'd taunted him in the medbay.

Now wasn't the time to shout things to upset the alien, but there was another way. She would get into his head.

Alex didn't know how to launch a telepathic attack. Every telepathic event so far had been her reacting to what either the Dark One or Vardis had started.

Thinking about what she didn't know wasn't going to get her and Roy out of this, though. Alex closed her eyes, took a deep breath, and concentrated on what she was trying to do. She needed to distract Vardis. Maybe if he thought he was somewhere else…

Alex focused on the planet she'd seen in his memory. She tried to build it up in the room. To make the vans and planes and tanks disappear. To see the mud dripping down the walls. To create a place as close to what she had seen in the alien's mind as she could.

When she thought she had a good mental image, she focused on sending it to Vardis. She imagined a flying dagger made of the images, aimed at his head.

Vardis stopped looking around and froze as if he'd been hit with another ice grenade. He let loose a scream as he grabbed the side of his head. "Stay out of my head!"

Alex felt his retaliation. It was like her skull was splitting open, but the pain passed quickly. Was that what she had just done to Vardis?

The alien hadn't come back with a telekinetic attack either. Alex's theory seemed right. Vardis was a stronger psychic than Alex too, but he couldn't use both powers at the same time. That meant he could be stopped.

Alex commed Roy. "Hey, he can't use telepathy and telekinesis at the same time. If I distract him, maybe we can get some good shots in."

Roy's voice came back. "You better get distracting, then."

As Alex was preparing to answer, the tank she was hiding behind rose into the air. The alien had found her.

Alex drew her plasma pistol and fired a few shots as she scurried to find somewhere else to hide while Vardis tore the tank apart. While she was fleeing, she imagined thousands of aliens like Vardis, all of them begging him not to kill them, their bodies broken and battered. She directed the thought toward him, again imagining a dagger hitting him in the forehead.

Vardis screamed again and dropped the shredded tank. As he clutched his forehead, he descended, then caught himself but didn't go back up.

Roy jumped toward him, aiming a flying kick at the alien.

Vardis recovered fast enough to catch Roy in midair and fling him away. The amount of force he used was noticeably less.

Alex was preparing to double around and attack when Vardis' riposte hit her.

The hangar disappeared.

Alex was at home in the living room. Her parents were on the couch. Their skin had been peeled back, and their eye sockets were empty. The room smelled like rotting flesh, and the smell was creeping up Alex's nose. She screamed and took a step back.

Her parents stood and shambled toward her, growling words under their breath that made no sense, for they had no tongues. Alex knew what they were saying anyway.

You did this. You did this to us.

Alex screamed and screamed and shut her eyes tight. When she opened them, she was back in the hangar, curled in a ball on the floor. As she got back to her feet, she saw Vardis flying at her.

He landed on top of her hard and wrapped his hands around her throat, his face inches away from hers.

Alex choked as she tried to get out of Vardis' grip. Even though she was panicking, Alex knew he had made a mistake. She reached up with her bionic arm and grabbed his neck with as much force as she could.

Vardis gasped for breath as he released her.

Alex flicked her wrist, drawing her scythe.

Before Alex could attack, Vardis pressed both hands to Alex's head. The air around Alex shimmered, then she felt the weight of a thousand jackhammers hit her in the forehead.

The ground beneath her skull broke apart from the sheer amount of force. It was all Alex could do to shield herself.

Roy hit Vardis from the side and knocked the alien off her. She rolled away, holding her head as blood poured from her nose.

Out of the corner of her eye, Alex saw that Roy wasn't letting up. He had grabbed the alien and pulled him to his feet. Roy punched him in the stomach, and as Vardis doubled over, the mech rider brought his elbow down on his neck.

Vardis stumbled back, raising his hands as if begging Roy to relent.

Roy cracked his knuckles and walked toward Vardis, but grabbed the side of his head and screamed in pain.

Vardis dashed forward, jumped up, and delivered a roundhouse kick to Roy's head, sending the rider into a pile of debris from one of Vardis' earlier attacks.

Then the alien lashed out with his telekinesis at Alex, hitting her in the chest.

Alex tumbled across the floor as Vardis lifted a tank into the air, positioning it right over her. He brought the tank down.

Alex reached out, trying to stop the tank from crushing her.

The tank froze in midair, vibrating from the stress of the two opposing psychics.

Roy slipped behind Vardis and put the alien in a half-Nelson.

The alien lost his focus, and Alex was able to move the tank far enough to be out of danger.

As Vardis struggled to get away from Roy, Alex rushed over and punched him in the face with her bionic arm. Vardis' body slumped, and Alex hammered the alien with another blow. His body went limp, although Roy continued to hold him up. "Finish him," he growled.

Alex looked at Vardis, who had blood trickling from his eyes. "I think he's finished."

Suddenly Vardis surged up, and the lights in the hangar went black. Alex felt herself tumbling, and she could no longer tell if she was in the real world or in the manipulation the alien had cast. Either way, she had been wrong. He was only getting started.

CHAPTER FOUR

"We can end this right now, Vardis! It doesn't have to be a fight!"

Alex was stalling. Even though she and Roy had gotten the jump on Vardis a couple of times during the fight, it was becoming obvious that he outclassed them. Every time Alex thought they had the alien, he tossed them off and kept going.

Chine was going to be needed for this one. Alex wasn't sure where he was, though. Roy had mentioned earlier that everyone had been evacuated. On top of that, Vardis was doing something to block communications.

Alex was able to reach Chine through a shared dream with Vardis when she was at home, though. The distance then had been greater, and she'd been under much more stress. If she'd contacted Chine then, she'd be able to do it now.

All Alex needed was for Vardis to focus on something other than killing her for a second. It was too hard to concentrate while dodging tanks.

"We both want the same thing—the end of the Dark One. There's no reason one of us has to die."

Vardis' psychic energy lashed out of his body, tearing through a helicopter at his right. "One of us isn't going to die. Both of you are."

The ground in front of Vardis was vibrating from the energy coming off his body.

Alex focused on Chine, searching for him and concentrating on her message. *Chine! I need you! Vardis is going to kill us!*

She put everything she had into it, and as she focused, her skin grew hot, just like in the dream space. Without warning, flames burst out over her skin and shot from her eyes. As suddenly as the flames had erupted, they disappeared.

Alex fell to the floor, drained. She could hardly keep her eyes open. This was the most energy she'd ever expended using the draconic fluid in her blood. It felt as if she'd used it up.

Roy stepped in front of Alex and aimed his pistols at Vardis. "You take another step this way, and you're gonna have a hole the size of a watermelon in your head, if there's anything left."

Vardis cackled as he floated into the air. "If you could have killed me, human, you would have. There's no need to lie to yourself."

Roy chuckled as he fired at Vardis, who waved away the blasts. "That's because I've been playing with a handicap. Didn't think I was going to have to bring out the big guns." He slammed his hands together, and the exo-suit linked his fingers. He aimed his index fingers at the alien as if they were a gun. "Bang."

The tips of Roy's index fingers began to give off a faint blue light, then a plasma blast the size of a small car burst out, pushing him back against Alex.

It went straight at Vardis, whose eyes widened in fear. He tossed up a psychic shield as the plasma blast engulfed him.

Roy ran over to Alex and helped her to her feet. "Come on, we need to take cover. I don't know how much juice this thing has." He ran off, dragging Alex behind him. "Speaking of juice, how are you holding up?"

Alex leaned on the tank they were taking cover behind. "Tired, but I'll make it. I don't know if I can launch any more psychic attacks, but other than that, I can hang. What's the plan?"

"Uh, now that calling for backup is out of the question, I'm thinking we maybe try not dying?"

Vardis' scream rang through the hangar as the ground trembled. "He's losing it," Alex said. "He was referring to himself with the royal 'we' earlier, and you saw the look in his eyes. He's unhinged."

Roy was looking at the power reserves on his suit. "I was thinking it had more to do with the whole 'wipe out an entire universe without thinking twice' vibe but you know, to each their own."

"I reached out to Chine, but I don't know if he heard me, and I don't think I can do it again."

Roy nodded as he checked over the side of the tank for Vardis. "Guess it boils down to us. Thought you should know, you fight better than most people with three times your experience. And I don't think I've ever met a kid with as much heart as you."

Alex clapped Roy on the shoulder. "It's cute how you get all sentimental when you think you're going to die. Has Myrddin seen this side of you?"

"More than I'd like to admit. You ready? I'll go left—"

"I'll hit him from the right. Let's go."

They split up and went their respective ways. As Roy ran through the maze of broken tanks and helicopters, he kicked a truck-sized amount of debris out of his way, then stepped into the open.

A tank flew at Roy. He barely jumped out of the way, then rolled on the floor and fired two more plasma blasts in the direction the tank had come from.

Meanwhile, Alex circled around to flank Vardis while the alien's attention was on Roy.

Vardis was out in the open as well, but a psychic shield surrounded him—a giant bubble with a blue aura.

Alex assumed the shield would protect Vardis from psychic blasts and a reasonable amount of physical damage, but she wasn't planning on limiting it to "reasonable."

She charged him at full speed. While the alien was focused on deflecting Roy's plasma attacks, Alex leaped, whipped out her scythe, and slashed his shield open.

Vardis spun, catching Alex in midair. He pointed, and she slammed into the wall.

The rider tried to move, but she could not. It felt like a giant hand was squashing her into the wall. The alien wasn't holding back anymore.

Roy clapped his hands and fired another giant bolt of plasma.

This time Vardis was ready. He flew toward the ceiling, letting the plasma race past him. Then he yanked Roy into the air and held him there for a moment before slamming him into the ground.

Roy was trying to get to his feet when Vardis grabbed him again and flung him into the air before sending him back into the crater the first attack had created.

Vardis laughed loudly as white energy shot from his eyes.

Alex felt the alien's grip tightening around her body.

Once more, Roy was thrown into the air, only to be brought back down with enough force to break more than a few bones. This time Roy didn't get back up. He laid there, unconscious.

Alex struggled against Vardis' grip. "Get up, Roy! Get up!"

Vardis whirled to face Alex. "You can't get up when you're dead, human!"

Come on, Chine! If you're gonna get here, you better make it fast, Alex thought.

Vardis floated over to Alex and stopped nearly nose to nose with her. "Did you think you had a chance?"

Alex tried to fight off his attack, but her mind was too tired. "What now? You kill me and go to Middang3ard like nothing happened? Don't you think everyone is going to be suspicious if Roy and I don't show up?"

"You're in the medbay, and Roy said he was going to stay with you until you got better."

"And the staff here? They're just going to pretend they didn't see anything."

Vardis pressed his finger to Alex's forehead. "A few human minds to warp? Hardly a problem. You should know by now how fragile the human psyche is."

Alex tried to pull away from Vardis' finger. "Doesn't seem to be any more delicate than yours. Remember, I was in your head as well, and what I saw didn't look particularly strong."

Vardis winced at Alex's words. "Sometimes the things we see, they change us. We don't always get to choose how they do it. Change just happens."

The two looked at each other in silence for some time, Vardis' words hanging over Alex like an axe ready to fall on her neck. "You don't have to be changed like this," she offered.

Vardis turned away from the rider. "No, Alex. Someone must be strong enough to destroy the Dark One. I have that strength. I will not fail."

Alex felt a familiar warmth in the back of her head. It was Chine, but she was too tired to hear him. There was only a faint feeling of reassurance.

All Alex had to do was keep Vardis talking. She'd noticed the more she tugged at him, the harder time he seemed to have fighting. That was all this was now. He was distracted enough not to outright kill her and Roy. "What happened, Vardis?" Alex asked. "What really happened? Everything in your dreams, in your mind, was all jumbled. What did you see?"

The alien's shoulders relaxed and he sighed heavily. When he looked at Alex, his eyes had returned to normal, and his lower lip trembled. "I don't know. I really don't know. There are things I remember, but I'm not sure if they're my memories or if someone placed them there."

Alex wanted to take his words and throw them back in his face since apparently his mind could be broken as well, but that would have sent him into a rage that could easily end with him killing her right then and there. "Did someone tamper with your mind?"

Vardis' eyes hardened, and he looked like he was preparing to fly into another murderous rage. "It doesn't matter. I know the Dark One is real, and I know what he is capable of. That is all that matters. Goodbye, Alex."

Alex felt an invisible force tighten around her throat and wrists. She couldn't breathe. Her lungs were starting to burn, and everything was going fuzzy. "Wait, wait…"

Vardis crossed his arms and laughed harshly. "What for?"

The concrete wall Alex was pinned to exploded forward, throwing concrete and debris everywhere as Chine's head burst through the wall.

Vardis released her, and she fell to the floor.

Chine scooped Alex into his claws, where she lay limp for a moment, almost too weak to stand. *I am here, Alex.*

Alex shakily got to her feet, peering over Chine's claws at Vardis. *Glad to hear that. Now let's toast that bastard.*

Chine smiled toothily before loosing a blast of ether fire that consumed Vardis.

CHAPTER FIVE

Alex climbed up Chine's back and laid down, anchoring her feet to Chine so she wouldn't slide off. She felt ready to pass out. The battle had been grueling, but it was over. An extended stay in the medbay sounded heavenly.

Then she remembered Roy and sat bolt upright. "Chine, we need to check on Roy!"

The dragon swooped from the rafters to Roy's body. Alex forced herself up and jumped off Chine. She ran over to Roy's side and knelt next to him. "Roy! Roy!"

Roy rolled over, groaning loudly. His nose looked broken and was gushing blood, but other than that, he looked fine. "Don't know why we stopped using these suits. These things are tough."

Alex helped Roy sit up. "I don't think you can give the suit all the credit for you still breathing."

"Don't want to get too full of myself. My head is big enough." The mech rider leaned back, wincing from the pain, and looked at Chine. "Glad you made it when you did. I don't know what kind of steroids Vardis was on, but he was a monster to take down. Wouldn't be surprised if he would have given a couple of dragons a run for their money."

Alex took a seat next to Roy. She needed to be off her feet for a little bit. "Yeah, talk about good timing. How'd you find us, Chine?"

The dragon curled around Alex and Roy, smoke coming from his nostrils. *I've been looking since we were escorted off the base. It seemed odd that we all had to leave you while you were in the medbay. The captain who issued the order did not seem to be in complete control of his faculties.*

"Vardis probably inserted the idea into his head. The poor man most likely didn't know the idea was false."

Chine nodded slowly. *That was what I assumed after I remembered how strong a telepath you said Vardis was. It is not a simple task to rewrite someone's memory; even I can't do that. But once I had my doubts, I did not stop searching for your thoughts and your heart. Unfortunately, I'm too large to sneak away from a convoy without being missed.*

Alex laughed as she imagined the dragon trying to sneak through the Nest. "Yeah, that's hard to imagine. Where did you come from?"

Boundless and I were responsible for transporting the shard to a collider transport near here. There are a few military bases with designated colliders, this being one of them. From there, we were being taken to another base to get outfitted with augments in case something came up.

"How come Myrddin didn't have you go back to Middang3ard?"

Roy stepped in to answer that one. "He probably had them hang back in case something happened here. Boundless might be one of our best teams, but you aren't the only forces Myrddin has at his disposal. The shard's going to be heavily guarded. It would make more sense to have you guys stationed here in case something happened."

"Something like Vardis trying to kill you and me."

"Exactly."

Roy struggled to get to his feet, leaning on Alex's head like a makeshift cane while hauling himself upright. Then he reached down and helped her up. "Come on, we should check out the corpse. Knowing Myrddin, he'll probably want to ship it to some science department and have it dissected."

Alex thought of Abby getting Vardis' body in the mail and how much it would freak her out. "Oh, yeah, I imagine that'll make everyone's day."

The two of them walked over to where Vardis' corpse lay, followed by Chine, who towered over them.

Vardis' skin was burned to a crisp, and his body, which lay face-down looked like a broken toy. Alex thought the alien's corpse looked pathetic, almost tragic. The last few moments she'd shared with him had deeply confused her. Even though Vardis had the drive, it didn't seem like he understood where it was coming from. "I think someone tampered with Vardis' memories," Alex suggested.

Roy rolled Vardis' body over, knelt, and peered into the alien's eyes. "Wouldn't know how to tell. The only training I have in all this psychic stuff is protecting my mind. I don't know how to tell if someone has been or is currently being manipulated. Not my field of expertise. But even if he was, you gotta hand it to the guy. He sure as hell knew how to put up a fight."

"The Dark One is stronger than he was."

Roy looked over his shoulder at Alex, his face puzzled. "What do you mean?"

Alex thought it was obvious. "Vardis nearly tore us apart. If Chine hadn't gotten the jump on him, he might have been able to take him as well. He destroyed nearly twice as many ships as anyone else on the moon without breaking a sweat.

Vardis was the strongest being I've ever met. And the Dark One is supposed to be even stronger?"

Roy shrugged as he pulled out a cigar and lit it. "Yeah, he is stronger. Don't mean we can't beat him, though. You saw today that just because someone is tough, it doesn't mean they can't die. Vardis was the biggest, baddest son-of-a-gun you've fought so far. Now he's dead. The Dark One is next. Don't tell me you're starting to crack."

"No, it's not that. I just mean, if I was as strong as Vardis and knew there was something stronger than me out there, I might have been insane enough to want to use that shard. It would probably seem like a good idea."

Roy walked over to Alex and ruffled her hair. "Well, I'm glad you're not that strong, then. Come on, we should regroup with the rest of the team. They're probably wondering where Chine is by now. I'll radio for someone to take care of this. Comm should be back up with this asshat taken care of."

Roy pulled up his comm and frowned as he heard static. Then he pulled up his HUD menu. There was nothing there. "That's odd."

A massive psychic blast erupted, sending Alex, Roy, and Chine flying.

The cracked skin on Vardis' body started to peel back like the burned outer layer of a marshmallow. A slimy, slippery Vardis emerged from the thin layer of burned, dead skin. He looked untouched by Chine's fire attack.

The alien stretched out his hand as if he were getting used to his new skin. "I'm flattered that you had such kind things to say about me when you thought I was dead. It's fitting for warriors such as yourselves."

Without wasting another word, Vardis exploded into the sky, taking off in the direction Alex could only imagine led to the shard.

Alex rubbed her head, trying to shake away the ringing in her ears. She wasn't ready to keep fighting, but it didn't look like she had a choice. "Wait, Vardis is screwed. The shard is on Middang3ard. He can't get out of this realm without the collider, and that's where everyone is."

Roy was on his feet, and a vein in the side of his neck was bulging. "Unless he has got more tricks we don't know about, which wouldn't surprise me. I didn't think the S.O.B. could fake his death so easily. Why the hell did he do that?"

"Information. He obviously was so focused on the fight that he couldn't just lift the masterplan from our minds, so he waited until Chine conveniently explained everything that's happened since he attacked me. Vardis might be insane, but he knows how to plan."

"That makes our next step easy. I'm loading the coordinates into your anchor. Looks like he's far enough away that however he was jamming our comm isn't working anymore. Or maybe he just doesn't care."

Alex checked her anchor for the coordinates, and just as Roy had said, the jamming to their system was gone. "You want to talk to the team, and I'll focus on riding? I need to talk to Chine."

Alex climbed onto the dragon's back, and Roy followed. She anchored and then pulled out a pair of auxiliary reins that she attached to Chine's back and then handed to Roy. "Hold on," she advised. "I'll take it as slow as I can."

Roy waved away Alex's concerns. "Don't worry about me. This isn't the first time I've been on the back of a dragon without an anchor. Do you think they just shove us into mechs without bothering to teach us the basics? You fly as hard as you can."

Alex nodded and pulled back on her anchor, launching Chine into the air. *You can find him, right, Chine?*

Chine replied, *If we work together, we can find him. He's*

trying to cover his tracks by blocking his energy from us, but together, we can find him. Reach out, Dustling. Reach out and grab him.

Alex did just that, focusing on scanning the sky for Vardis' energy. She knew that energy intimately since it had tortured her mentally and tried to kill her for the last two hours. It shouldn't be difficult to find.

The rider and dragon searched for a little bit before Alex picked up a trace. She zeroed in on it, directing Chine to fly after the flicker. "Hey, Roy, you get in touch with everyone yet?"

Roy's voice came over Alex's comm. "Yeah, I did. It's going to take them a little time to get prepared, though. The facility's only makeshift. Most of the dragon hardware they have still needs to be set up, and Boundless is going to have to bring every weapon that they can get their hands on to this fight."

Alex was about to answer Roy when she felt a sharp pain near the back of her skull. Then her mind erupted in agony, but not the sort she felt from Vardis' attacks. This was much different. It was as if a single thought were repeating as often and loudly in Alex's head as possible.

She knew exactly what it was.

The Dark One.

Alex stopped trying to fight it and let the Dark One in. The world around her faded away, and she was in the dark place with a thin sliver of light in the distance. The thought was coming from the light. "He comes for the shard," the Dark One growled.

Alex wanted to roll her eyes. She couldn't believe this was why the Dark One had invaded her mind. "You're not telling me anything I don't already know."

"Have you rethought my proposition?

"Uh-uh, what did we talk about when it came to names? Use mine."

"Alex. What is your decision?"

Alex hadn't thought about the Dark One's promise since he made it. Something had appealed to her about it, and she was starting to think that was because of the Dark One's influence. Since then, she'd grown stronger, strong enough to ward it off unconsciously. "I'll keep Vardis from using the weapon, but I'm not giving it to you, and I have no desire whatsoever to join your army. I'm going to destroy you."

"I advise you to—"

"I'm done with this."

Alex cut the link, violently forcing the Dark One from her mind. It surprised her as much as it must have surprised him.

Suddenly Alex was back in the real world, riding Chine, who had taken over during his rider's brief lapse. She looked down at her anchor, which told her they were only a couple of minutes from the other base. Vardis might already be there, but it didn't matter. He hadn't beaten her yet. Why would this time be any different?

CHAPTER SIX

B y the time they arrived, the base's alarms were going off. Even from far off, Alex could see that a huge chunk of the base had been destroyed. Vardis had found the shard.

They landed near the makeshift stables, where Team Boundless was trying to prep their dragons for the counteroffensive.

Alex jumped off Chine as her team ran up to greet her.

Jim gave Alex a hug, holding her as tight as he could. "It's good to see you made it out of there all right. We've been trying to get in touch with the base since we left. Everyone just assumed it was a communication malfunction. We had a couple of people from the base tell us it was. It must have all been part of Vardis' plan."

Brath's arms were folded, and he was stewing. "Yeah, it looks like the asshole pulled the wool over all of our eyes. Even if we didn't trust him, I don't think any of us thought he was going to try something like this. Getting the shard transported and everyone to move to a base that hardly runs was a stroke of genius."

Jollies flittered to Alex's shoulder and landed on it. "We

were worried about you after the explosion. You are okay, right?"

Alex rubbed the back of her head, which had been hurting since the Dark One invaded her mind. "Yeah, I'll live. I'm only tired. Vardis has been drawing this out for a long time. It's like he doesn't get tired."

Gill, who was still working on setting up the augment station, called over his shoulder, "He does seem to be on a very different level than we once thought. He's already removed the shard and left with it, and we're stuck here, prepping for a fight that might very well be over by the time we leave. Got any idea about what to do next?"

Alex crouched as she thought about what her next step was going to be. If she was able to track Vardis to this base, maybe she'd be able to do the same when she was in Middang3ard. The alien's energy was unmistakable. "Guess the first step is to find out how bad the damage is. See if we can find out where he went from the collider logs. Roy and I will check it out. You guys keep getting ready for the fight."

The team went back to their duties as Alex and Roy headed for the collider. They didn't need to know the layout of the base. All they had to do was follow the path of destruction Vardis had left.

From the looks of it, he had torn through the base looking for the shard, which had been held in a special containment area.

Alex and Roy walked past the destroyed containment area. Wounded soldiers were being attended to by medics, but there didn't seem to be any casualties.

The riders followed the wreckage Vardis had left in his wake. It wasn't long until they reached the collider, which was still running, a portal open on the teleportation pad. "That can't be good," Alex murmured as she and Roy ascended the railing. "Aren't those supposed to close after they've been used?"

Roy opened the log. "Yeah, they close instantly. They can't be kept open."

Alex stared at the portal, trying to make sense of what she was looking at. "Do most people know that?"

"What do you mean?"

"That the portals always close. Would someone who's unfamiliar with them know they don't remain open when they're not in use?"

Roy continued to look through the list of potential coordinates. "I don't see why they would."

"This isn't real, not the way we think it is. Vardis is playing another trick on us. What was the last place the teleporter accessed?"

"Looks like the Wasps' Nest. Vardis probably went there to set off the shard. There's a lot of magical energy to draw from there. The kin would probably love that."

Alex shook her head as she came over to look at the console. "No, I don't think so. Vardis said they were elementals, and magic isn't an element, it's energy. The shard probably wouldn't work there. It's another distraction Vardis put up for us, just like that portal. Which isn't really there."

Roy looked at the portal and then to Alex. "You sure about that? Because I'm pretty sure I see a portal."

"If it really were an open portal, don't you think there would be technicians trying to shut it down? If the system was broken that badly, this whole base would be in danger."

Roy nodded in understanding. "He's messing with our minds again."

Alex shut her eyes, focusing her tired mind on dispelling the telepathic fog Vardis had placed over the room. Or maybe he had inserted it into their minds, along with everyone else's at the base. Was Vardis strong enough to affect hundreds of people at the same time?

Roy pointed at one of the ceiling's corners. "He destroyed the cameras in here as well."

"Hold on. I'm trying to concentrate."

Alex turned her focus inward, trying to find anything that didn't belong. She had the same feeling as when she'd tried to remember any information about her parents after Vardis' attack. The sensation was recognizable.

There it was—the telepathic schism.

Alex slashed at it with her mind and did the same to Roy's, which caused him to yelp. "Oh, crap, you weren't joking," he said.

When Alex opened her eyes, the portal was gone. In its place was what looked like a small tear in the fabric of space and time. It distorted everything around it, crackling with the same energy that came off of Vardis. It was the same energy Alex had seen when the grenade in the back of the van exploded. "It's a psychic mine," Alex explained. "He was hoping we'd try to use the fake portal and set it off."

"Hm, that's ominous. Any idea how to get rid of it?"

"None. You should call someone to take care of that before we leave. Now, if you were going to go to one place that had unlimited elemental potential in all Middang3ard, where would it be?"

"They mentioned that volcano, and Vardis was there for that briefing, I think. If he's anywhere, that's where I'd bet."

Alex pointed to the console. "Hit the coordinates and let's go."

Roy started searching the console. "No collider opens there. We're going to have to travel some of the way."

Chine flew through the hole in the ceiling and landed near the dragon teleportation section of the collider. *Are we ready?*

Roy hit the teleportation terminal, and a portal ripped into their world. "We are now," Alex said as she ran to the dragon. She jumped onto his back and anchored herself as Roy followed, then they flew into the portal.

Alex felt herself tumbling through the portal, watching thousands of stars race past as she was pulled between the realms.

They landed on a teleportation portal in Middang3ard in the middle of a base not very different from the one they just left, except the technology was much more advanced.

Alex sent the coordinates they had used to the rest of Boundless and ordered them to come through to Middang3ard and head for the volcano as soon as possible. Alex, Roy, and Chine were going to find Vardis and try to stall him.

The attendants at the collider stared at the dragon in confusion. "Uh, excuse me," one of them said. "You weren't cleared for teleportation."

Alex leaned over his neck. "I know, I'm sorry, but it's an emergency. I'm Alex Bound. I should have full clearance."

The attendant pulled up his HUD menu and scanned it for a few seconds before nodding and giving Alex a thumbs-up. "Did anyone else come through here recently?" Alex asked. "Someone without the proper clearance?"

The attendant looked at Alex, scrunching his face as he thought, as did the rest of the attendants. They looked like they were trying to remember something but couldn't quite get there. "Uh, no, no one else came through," the attendant finally said.

Alex looked at Roy, who was starting to figure it out too. "Vardis must have tampered with their memories."

Chine rolled his shoulders uncomfortably. *He was able to cast an illusion on you from between realms and distort the memo-*

ries of those here as well. I've never seen a telepath that strong before.

"You worried, Chine?"

Slightly. But what else is there to do?

The dragon was right. Alex pulled up on her anchor and sent him into the skies of Middang3ard to chase Vardis.

CHAPTER SEVEN

I t had been so long since Alex had been in Middang3ard that she hardly recognized it. She was captivated by the skies, the first ones she had ever seen, in passing as she was taken to Middang3ard.

In many ways, Middang3ard felt more like home than Earth ever could since she'd seen Middang3ard in VR for such a long time. Until she'd gotten her eyes, Middang3ard had been all she'd ever seen, other than her textbooks and holographic lessons.

This was what was at stake.

Vardis had tried to pose his offer as having Alex destroy a place she didn't care about, but he hadn't known that Alex felt more at home on Middang3ard than anywhere else.

Alex quickly pushed her feelings aside. Nostalgia wasn't going to help her. What was important now was getting to Vardis as fast as possible. She drove her anchor forward to push Chine to maximum speed.

It was obvious that Vardis was going to make it to the volcano before they did; nothing could be done about that.

But Vardis was crafty, so there was going to be something waiting for them when they arrived.

Alex ran through the different scenarios she could anticipate Vardis hitting her with. There was telekinetic energy. Then there was telepathy, either Vardis trying to influence her thoughts and perspective, or attempting to envelop her in a full-on psychic attack, pulling at her memories to confuse her about reality.

Any of those options, Alex felt like she could handle. She'd already experienced them firsthand.

She tried to lock onto Vardis' energy. Even from so far away, she could sense it. He *was* heading to the volcano. From what she could tell, he hadn't arrived yet. Hopefully, that meant he wouldn't be able to set up a good defense.

Even though Vardis was insane, there was something almost admirable about how much he was willing to throw away, to sacrifice for his single-minded desire to kill the Dark One. Alex wondered if she'd ever be capable of that kind of conviction.

Then she wondered whether she would ever want that kind of resolute determination, the ability to kill billions of people. She would never do anything like that, but she was starting to see why someone would.

They were coming up on the volcano.

It sat in the middle of an island that was mostly covered with jungle. The island was the size of a small country, and there didn't seem to be any fauna on it. The volcano looked angry, ready to explode at any given moment. Smoke plumed from the open chasm in the fiery mountain.

As Chine neared the island, Roy asked, "This is where we're supposed to be fighting?"

Alex didn't bother answering. She was still wondering why Vardis hadn't started using the shard yet. There was no way they'd beaten him to the island. She could feel his energy lighting up the area. "Yeah, something is going to happen here."

Rather than go to the mouth of the volcano, Alex decided to land Chine at its base. She and Roy got off the dragon and stared at the volcano they were going to have to scale. "Any reason you decided to land us as far from the fight as possible?" Roy asked.

Alex hardly heard him. She was busy tending the augments that were still on the dragon. He'd been outfitted with the bare minimum for a fight, probably having guided one of the military personnel on how to attach them. "Chine needs to be looked after," Alex explained. "I'm not taking him into a fight until I do that."

She got to work draining the draconic fluid from the augments. There was a build-up of fluid, but it didn't take long. Alex finished by plunging her anchor into Chine's spine and absorbing the rest of the fluid. "He's waiting for us," she said. "He could have summoned the kin by now, but he hasn't. I think he sees us as on par with the Dark One. We're one more step he has to take before he can get rid of him."

Roy clicked his tongue as he checked the energy on his exo-suit. "Sounds like this guy is getting crazier by the moment."

Alex was looking up the side of the volcano. It wouldn't take long to scale it with Chine, but she was worried about what she was going to find when she got to the summit. Whatever Vardis had was going to hit hard, and she wasn't certain if she was ready for it.

CHAPTER EIGHT

The three started to make their way up the side of the volcano. Roy wanted to fly Chine straight up it, thinking they were wasting valuable time, but Alex convinced him that this was the wiser tack. She couldn't explain why, but it had something to do with her connection to Vardis' mind.

Vardis' thoughts were drenching the volcano. It was a physical presence. All three of the interlopers felt the effect.

At first, the feeling was subtle. Alex felt it as mild irritation without knowing what she was annoyed by. Neither Roy nor Chine were talking, yet her mind was replaying nearly everything Roy had said over the last few minutes, then days, then months, looking for something to be bothered by.

Alex saw Roy casting disapproving glances at her. She didn't need him to say anything, nor did she need to read his mind. It was all over his face.

She wasn't sure if that was the reason for the silence. Was Roy judging her? Did he not think she was capable of handling this?

That was when Alex noticed the oddity of her feelings. There was no reason for her to be focusing on those things. For one, negativity wasn't going to help. Second, she was looking for issues that weren't there.

Alex stopped walking and stared at the smoke rising from the tip of the volcano. "You guys feel that, right?"

Roy sat down on a rock, wiping sweat from his brow. He looked like he was ready to snap at Alex, but he held his tongue. "You going to explain what you're talking about?"

"How annoyed are you with me right now?"

Roy slowly shook his head and he avoided Alex's eyes. "I don't think that's appropriate to be talking about right now. I'd rather not be talking to you at all, so there you go."

"Do you know why? What did I do to annoy you?"

Roy went red and stumbled over his words. "Hey! I didn't bring it up. You're the one—"

"No, I mean, can you remember anything specifically."

Roy furrowed his brow as he thought about Alex's question. "Actually, I can't. I can't think of one reason why I'd be pissed at you. I mean, I should feel the complete opposite."

"It's Vardis; he's messing with our heads again. Like I said before, he's not going to be content with activating the shard. He wants to torture us."

Roy groaned and leaned back against the rock he was sitting on. "Okay, I did PsyOps training, but it was nothing like this. Most people would have burned out by now. How does this guy have the energy to keep this up so long?"

Chine chimed in. *His race must have a propensity for psychic powers, and he is probably considered strong by their standards.*

Alex hadn't taken her eyes off the black smoke coming from the volcano. It was thicker than the clouds surrounding the volcano. "It's just going to get worse the farther up we go, and I know he has more planned."

Roy stood and wiped away sweat again. "I liked the guy a lot better when he was just hurling tanks at us."

Alex chuckled for the first time in what felt like hours. "Honestly, that was easier to deal with. Come on, we should keep moving. I'll do what I can to force Vardis out of our heads."

They continued up the mountain, cutting through a thick swath of jungle, still keeping quiet as Alex attempted to unhook Vardis' grasp from their minds. It was tiring work. At first, Alex felt like she was stumbling around in the dark, but over time, she got a feel for it and reached in with telepathic fingers, searching for whatever stood out and slowly prying the foul thoughts out of her mind and Roy's.

Alex didn't bother with the dragon. He had enough experience with telepaths to guard himself.

The whole process was exhausting. They'd only been walking for thirty minutes, and Alex already felt like she could pass out. "We need to find water," she moaned.

Roy was dripping with sweat, and he nodded and pulled up a map on his HUD. "Hm, looks like there's some a little way from here. And guess what? Our comms are still working. Vardis must be prepared for a fight."

"He better be. Let's get that water."

Roy moved to the front of their group and led them off the path they were following. He headed south until they came across a clear spring that was filled by a stream trickling from the side of the mountain. It looked like an oasis and reminded Alex of the date Jim had taken her on.

She sat down by the spring and dipped her head under the water. Its coolness was beyond refreshing. Alex pulled her head back and flipped her hair out of her face before cupping her hands and drawing water to drink.

Roy knelt next to Alex and started guzzling water as if he were a wild animal. Finally, he sat back and burped loudly, then he reached into the chest pocket of his exo-suit and pulled out two protein bars. He tossed one to Alex. "Haven't had a field mission like this in a long time. Forgot how exhausting this crap is without a mech."

Alex pointed at Roy's exo-suit. "Isn't that helping?"

Roy shook his head. "It's off now. Trying to conserve energy. Right now, it just feels like I'm wearing a hunk of metal."

"We should get going."

Alex stood to leave but stopped cold. There was something at the bottom of the spring that looked like a body. "You see that?"

Roy peered into the water, and without hesitation, leaped into the spring.

Alex watched Roy descend into the water, trying to figure out why she felt like she was frozen with fear. "Chine, what's going on?"

The dragon didn't answer.

Alex turned to see what was wrong with him. The dragon was on his back, twitching violently and breathing heavily. "Chine! *Chine!*" Alex screamed as she ran to the dragon. "Are you—"

Chine loosed a heavy sigh and went limp.

Alex shook his shoulder, tears welling in her eyes, but it didn't wake him. She watched his chest slowly stop rising. "Chine!"

Roy called to Alex. He was making his way out of the water, holding a body. It was Jim, all bloated and blue-green from rot, his eyes empty sockets that mud had collected in. As Roy struggled with Jim's body, he tripped and fell forward. The corpse rolled in front of Alex.

Alex backed away. "It's not real. It's not real. *None of this is real!*"

Jim's rotten hand grabbed Alex's ankle and clawed its way

up her leg as she screamed and tried to kick him off. "We're all going to die, Alex," he moaned. "We're all going to die today!"

The spring's water turned dark red and exploded upward like a tornado of blood. It was pulling Jim back into it, and he wasn't letting go of Alex's leg. She fell into the mud as Jim was dragged back into the water. "We're all going to die, and it's all your fault. All your fault. *ALL YOUR FAULT!*"

Jim was halfway into the blood lake now, his bony hands digging into Alex's leg.

She knew that this was an illusion. That didn't change the fact that she was trapped in it. She couldn't shake the smell of Jim's decaying flesh or the bloody water she was being pulled into. What if she died in one of these illusions? Would she wake up as from a dream, or would she die in the real world?

"ALL YOUR FAULT! ALL YOUR FAULT!"

"I know!" Alex screamed. "I know it will be!"

Jim stopped chanting and stared at Alex with a slack jaw.

Alex kicked the corpse in the face, breaking the skull in half. "I know it'll be my fault. I accept that."

The illusion disappeared. Alex was sitting in front of the spring, Roy and Chine drinking water at her side. She had no idea how long she'd been out. "Come on, we need to keep going."

Roy could see the stress on Alex's face, but he said nothing.

Alex climbed onto Chine's back as they continued to make their way up the side of the mountain. She needed rest more than anything else. The attacks from Vardis had worn her down. Even though they weren't real, they were draining, which must be Vardis' goal. A war of attrition.

She couldn't even take a quick nap. The dream world was just as dangerous as being awake, or maybe more so. The most she could do was let her body rest, close her eyes, and let herself drown in darkness for a little bit.

Chine and Roy cut up the side of the volcano, taking the most direct route possible. The dragon took point, cutting down any trees in their way with his claws, while Alex drifted in and out of sleep, trying to keep her eyes open and failing miserably.

Roy watched Alex fitfully trying to rest. "You think she's going to be okay?"

Chine continued without breaking speed. *I'm watching over her.*

"I figured, but that's not my question. Is she going to be okay?"

Chine sighed, emitting a plume of black smoke. *Her mind is young. The sort of attacks she's gone through with such regularity would have driven you insane. You'd be a slobbering, incoherent mess. She is not. This will not be what breaks Alex Bound. The fight ahead, though? I do not know if any of us will be okay.*

Roy nodded as he jogged to catch up with the dragon. "Not worried about that. We take each fight as it comes. I just want to know if she'll be okay until then."

She is strong. She will survive.

Roy looked at Chine. "Hey, we've never talked before. Are you psychic or something?"

Chine raised one of his scaly brows.

"Never mind," the mech rider muttered. "Stupid question."

After another twenty minutes of hiking, they neared the summit. Chine stopped and jerked his shoulders to wake Alex up.

Alex slid off Chine's back and landed on her feet in front of Roy. She was smiling.

Roy couldn't help smiling back. "What's got you looking so happy?"

Alex went over to the dragon and started to drain the draconic fluid from his claws. "Had a dream, a pretty good one. I snapped Vardis' neck. It felt good, and I'm pretty sure Vardis wasn't responsible for that vision. It was all mine."

She leaped onto Chine's back and anchored herself. "Let's save the universe."

CHAPTER NINE

As they flew, the air was thick with sulfur. It didn't take long to reach the top.

The maw didn't merely contain lava. There were sections of rock floating in it. They had to be constructs since there was no way anything natural could withstand the heat.

Alex felt like she was going to pass out until her uniform compensated for the heat. She looked at Roy, who was obviously struggling in his exo-suit. When he saw her worried face, he said, "Don't worry, I'm still conserving power. I'm not going to faint on you. So, you think we got what it takes to end this?"

Alex wasn't certain she did. Vardis had fought both Roy and her for the better part of the day. "We're going to need reinforcements."

"Already called them in, Team Boundless and more. All we have to do is survive for half an hour. You think that's doable?"

Alex nodded. "There's a reason he hasn't activated the shard yet. He needs his strength to summon the kin. It's not tech, it's psychic. It must be. Same reason he didn't go down the mountain to finish us off. He's exhausted. That's why he resorted to attacking me telepathically—to wear me down because he's in the same state.

"Glad to finally get some good news."

Chine banked around the volcano, coming in to land.

Alex could see Vardis. He was sitting on one of the stone platforms in the volcano's throat. The alien's legs were crossed as he meditated, the shard floating in front of him.

When Alex landed, she walked down the length of Chine's back and drew her scythe. "Vardis! Let's finish this!"

Vardis opened one of his eyes, bemused. He got to his feet, moving the shard behind him. "And here I was thinking you wouldn't have the courage to face me again. Have you come to see how the Dark One finally meets his end?"

Alex twirled her scythe as she yawned. "The trash-talk is getting boring. Let's get to it already." She leaned forward, driving Chine at him.

Vardis seemed surprised by Alex's straightforward attack but threw up a psychic shield at the last minute as Chine collided with him.

The two flew backward as Chine bit the shield, and Vardis' eyes were wide with fear.

Alex decreased the strength of her anchor to Chine and ran down the dragon's neck. She raised her scythe and swung it at Vardis, hitting his shield, which held up.

The alien stretched his arms out, exploding the shield into a psychic shockwave that knocked Alex and Chine away as Roy leaped off the dragon onto one of the platforms.

Once Vardis had space, he smiled sarcastically. "Who would have thought a nap would restore so much of your vigor?"

Alex rolled her shoulders, cracking her joints before stretching and touching her toes. "You wanted a fight, I wanted to make sure your last one was worth remembering."

"Oh, it will be one for the books."

Vardis vanished, reappearing right in front of Alex, on top of Chine. He formed a psychic ball in his hand and slammed it into her chest.

The force of the blast sent Alex skidding across the dragon's back. She grabbed Chine's tail and flipped herself back up. Then she dashed at Vardis, relying on her speed, and decked him in the face, knocking the alien to his knees.

Vardis didn't even need to catch his breath. He reached out to his side and pulled Chine's wing up with telekinesis.

Chine veered hard to the left, briefly losing control.

Alex's anchor adjusted and pinned her feet to Chine's back as the dragon did a barrel roll, Vardis still pulling on the dragon's wing.

Alex drew her plasma pistol and fired two shots as Vardis raised his hand to form a shield. That was enough to let Chine regain control of his wing and straighten out.

From below, Roy fired a giant plasma bolt at Vardis, who simply raised his hand and dispersed the attack.

Alex reached out telekinetically and pushed Vardis back a few feet. It was enough to surprise him, and that was all Alex needed. She tossed her scythe at the alien, who ducked the attack.

Before Vardis could regain his balance, Alex was in his face. She kicked him in the chest, which knocked the wind out of him, then brought her elbow down on Vardis' neck.

He hit Chine's back and rolled over, then swung his feet around and tripped Alex.

Now she could see Vardis' plan: stay on Chine's back and basically nullify the dragon. That also cut off how much Roy was able to help, greatly reducing his shots so he didn't hit the dragon. It was a good plan, but Alex wasn't going to let it stand.

As Vardis stood back up, Alex ran at him and delivered a

flying drop-kick that pushed Vardis to the edge of Chine's back. Alex also pushed the alien telekinetically, sending him flying off.

Vardis caught himself in mid-air and rose, drawing his energy into a ball that he tossed at the dragon.

Alex pulled up on her anchor and yanked Chine into the air, and the blast flew past them. Then Alex leaned forward, driving the dragon at Vardis.

Chine launched an ether attack at Vardis, who swung to the right to avoid being caught in it. As he tried to reposition himself, Roy fired another massive plasma blast that hit him in the back.

The alien screamed as he turned to Roy. "Pathetic."

Vardis rocketed at Roy, slamming into the rock in front of the human. He grabbed the mech rider by the throat and lifted him into the air.

Alex drove Chine toward Vardis, looking through her augment menu as quickly as possible to see what Chine had loaded. She launched flash-freeze grenades at the island Roy and Vardis were on.

Vardis raised his hand, stopping the grenades in mid-air and causing them to explode.

Alex hadn't expected the trick to work on Vardis twice, which was why she was already sailing toward him, her scythe high above her head. She slashed through the wall of ice that had formed and kicked Vardis in the face.

Vardis stumbled back, but before Alex could attack again, he grabbed her head and sent a powerful telepathic attack screeching through it, causing her to shriek as pain ripped through her brain.

Disoriented, Alex stumbled back, nearing the edge of the slab she was on.

Chine swooped behind Alex and grasped her with one set of claws, reaching for Roy with the other.

Vardis stepped between Chine and Roy, raising his hand and stopping the dragon midway.

The dragon tried to force his way through Vardis' power but couldn't.

Roy took the opportunity to leap to an island farther away from Vardis and fired two shots that Vardis deflected easily.

Chine soared into the air, putting some space between him and Vardis as Alex composed herself.

The world stopped shaking, and she focused again. Alex looked down at her dragon anchor—another ten minutes before their reinforcements arrived.

Alex commed Team Boundless. "Hey, where are you guys?"

Jollies answered, "We've just come through the collider transport. We're heading your way as fast as possible, and we're bringing the big guns."

"Thank God. I don't know how much longer we're going to be able to hold out."

"Just keep fighting."

A psychic blast rocketed toward Alex and she pulled Chine to the left, barely avoiding it.

Vardis seemed satisfied with pushing Alex and Chine back and turned his attention to Roy, who was still trying to put distance between him and Vardis. The alien flew at Roy, psychic blasts forming in both of his palms.

Roy braced for the impact and Vardis hit him hard, sending him into the wall of the volcano.

The alien grabbed Roy by the throat to keep him from falling into the lava. Vardis' eyes were white and wild with crazed energy. He formed another psychic blast in one of his palms and slowly pushed it into Roy's face.

Chine came in from the right and slashed Vardis across

the side, which knocked him off the rider. As Roy fell, Chine scooped him up and flew away.

Alex disengaged her anchor enough to leap into Chine's palm.

Roy was coughing up blood and his arm was broken, a piece of bone jutting from the exo-suit. Still, he was trying to get to his feet.

Alex rested her hand on Roy's chest and held him down. "You need to sit this one out."

Roy continued to try to stand, shaking his head adamantly. "I'm not leaving you to do this alone."

Alex looked at Chine and pointed to the rim of the volcano. "I'm not alone. I've got my dragon."

Chine placed Roy a little past the rim of the volcano, safely away from the lava leaking from cracks in the slope.

Vardis screamed with rage within the volcano.

Alex shouted in reply. "Don't worry, we're coming for you!"

Chine rose into the air and headed back into the volcano.

Vardis had descended into the heart of the volcano and was using his psychic powers to twist the lava to his desires. As Chine stormed toward him, the alien waved his hand and sent a glob of lava at Chine.

Brace yourself, Dustling.

Chine folded his wings over his head, blocking the lava from getting to Alex while allowing his body to absorb the blow. He hit Vardis hard, knocking the alien down, and held him beneath his feet. *Fool! I was born of fire!*

Vardis smiled menacingly. "Oh, were you?" He gave a rage-filled scream and shattered the island that Chine held him under, covering himself in a thin psychic shield as he fell into the lava, Chine toppled after him as Alex scrambled to get off the dragon's back.

Vardis pulled the closest islands into the lava as well,

leaving Alex nowhere to go as the alien continued trying to pull Chine into the lava.

Chine, in a last-ditch effort, reached out of the lava and grabbed Alex. He flung her toward another island.

Alex hit the island and rolled across its surface, then drew her scythe, and slammed it into the stone to keep herself from going off the edge.

Vardis was already back in the air. He was pulling rocks from the side of the mountain and throwing them at Chine to keep the dragon from getting out of the lava.

Alex knew that even if Chine could handle being exposed to lava, he wasn't a red dragon. The lava was going to eat through all his augments and eventually his skin as well.

Not knowing what else to do, Alex concentrated on a mental spear. She hurled it at Vardis, infusing it with every hurtful thing she could remember from his past.

Vardis grabbed his head and swayed to the side. It was enough to let Chine pull himself out of the lava and fly to Alex.

The dragon landed behind his rider and collapsed in a heap of flames. Alex ran to him, only briefly deterred by the flames. She took a deep breath and plunged through them to throw her arms around Chine's neck. *Hey, buddy, are you okay?*

Chine groaned as he tried to lift his head. *Just need a moment.*

Alex looked at Chine's claws and could see he was bleeding draconic fluid heavily. She plunged her anchor into the claw augment to draw out as much of his pain as possible.

The feeling was almost unbearable. The psychic link between Chine and Alex was strong enough that she felt all of his pain, coupled with the pain of absorbing the super-heated fluid into the anchor.

But it wasn't only going to the anchor. Alex felt the draconic fluid entering her blood.

A boulder smashed into the island Alex and Chine were on, nearly hitting the dragon in the head.

Vardis was floating above them with four boulders revolving around him, preparing to launch another attack.

Alex drew her scythe and slashed one of the boulders as it flew at Chine. "Leave him alone! He's done! Can't you see that?"

Vardis cackled madly as he prepared to throw another boulder. "Is he?"

Behind Alex, Chine whimpered softly.

That sound was too much for Alex, and something in her snapped.

Her blood started to boil.

Everything went red, and Alex reached out with everything she had to pull Vardis to her.

Black flames erupted across Alex's body as her blood metabolized the draconic fluid in her blood, boosting her energy exponentially.

Vardis was pulled to Alex, incapable of stopping her.

The alien hit the island face-first.

Alex, eyes burning pure black, grabbed him by the back of the neck and raised him into the air, then kicked him in the stomach with a combination of brute strength and telekinetic energy.

Vardis spit up blood as his eyes went wide with pain.

Alex slammed her bionic fist into the top of Vardis' skull, smashing him into the ground. Then she climbed on top of him, blind with rage, and started punching him in the head. The air was filled with the sound of bones cracking.

Her fist blazed with black energy as it crashed down on Vardis' head again and again.

Alex didn't know how long she'd been striking him. She

didn't stop until she heard Chine's voice in her head. *They're here. Reinforcements are here.*

The flames disappeared and Alex ran to Chine, then leaped onto his back and attached her anchor. "Can you fly?"

Yes, Dustling.

Alex pulled up on her anchor, and Chine took off. A circle of riders ringed the rim of the volcano. All of Boundless was there, along with more than twenty mech riders, their weapons trained on Vardis.

Alex reached for the shard and pulled it to her, clutching it tightly under her arm as she and Chine got out of range. "Hit him with everything you got!" she shouted.

Boundless and the rest of the riders didn't have to be told twice. They unloaded energy projectiles, breath attacks, and missiles at the alien.

Vardis weakly threw up a shield, but it did nothing.

A small explosion erupted in the volcano as each attack landed on Vardis.

Once the smoke settled, Alex could see Vardis' body. She, along with everyone else, watched to see if the alien was going to stand.

He didn't move.

Alex commed her team and the rest of the riders. "I'm going to check and see if he's done." She guided Chine down to Vardis' body, jumped off, and walked over to the alien.

Smoke was still coming off the body. She knelt beside him and put her finger to his neck to feel for a pulse.

Vardis' hand shot up and grabbed her arm. He weakly tilted his head and glared at her. The hate and anger in his eyes would probably have killed Alex if the alien had any more strength left. "You had your chance," he spat.

Alex wrenched her arm away from him. "No, *you* had *yours*. We could have worked together. Your blind desire for vengeance did this."

Vardis started laughing, hacking up blood. "Oh, Alex, it was so much more than vengeance. Do you know what it is like to not know your own mind? To have it broken so you do not even know who you are anymore?"

Alex stood up, looking disdainfully at the alien. "I got pretty close to finding out because of you. You've become everything you hated."

Vardis was still laughing softly. "What are you going to do with the shard?"

"Put it someplace safe. I know how dangerous it is. We're never going to let anyone like you get their hands on it again."

Vardis continued coughing blood and rolled over on his side, glaring at Alex from one of his eyes. "You might think so, but I have a parting gift for you—one you will no doubt enjoy."

Vardis closed his eyes, his body thrumming with energy. A shockwave emerged from him and spread through the volcano, but it did not stop there. It reverberated across Middang3ard and into all nine of the realms.

"Let them see you for what you really are."

The vision hit her with the force of a megaton bomb. It nearly obliterated her memories.

Then she felt something between her and the vision. Alex wasn't certain what had put itself between her and Vardis' illusion, but whatever it was, it was strong.

The vision was not meant for her. It was meant for the rest of Middang3ard.

She could see herself in the medbay. Roy was there. There was a knock on the door, and Roy answered it. Vardis asked to come in, and Roy allowed it.

As soon as Vardis stepped into the room, Alex's eyes went wild with hate. Ether flames burst across her body. She flew into a rage and attacked Vardis.

The two began their battle through the military base, Vardis fleeing from Alex and her giving chase. She killed two nurses in her rage. Nothing was going to stop her. Finally, Vardis managed to knock her out to give himself enough time to escape.

Roy came to Alex's side, asking why she had attacked Vardis. Alex gave no answer but turned on Roy instead, knocking him out. Then she chased Vardis, finding him at the collider.

Vardis went through the collider, and Alex went after him. She followed him to the volcano, where he was trying to place the weapon. He explained that Alex was wrong about it destroying the whole universe, that it was a mind trick the Dark One had played on her.

Alex watched herself telling Vardis that there was no trick, that the Dark One had promised her power and she'd accepted it. She told him she was betraying Middang3ard.

Roy came over the rim of the volcano. He begged Alex not to go over to the Dark One's side. Alex shouted that it was the only way she could save her life. The Dark One was going to win. She wasn't going to become a slave.

Alex attacked Roy with Chine, nearly killing him. Then she turned her wrath on Vardis.

The mech and dragonriders arrived as Alex was beating Vardis, who was begging for his life. He promised that if Alex would just let him use the weapon, the Dark One would be destroyed, and she wouldn't have anything to fear.

Alex climbed on top of the alien and strangled him to death.

The vision ended, and Alex stumbled away from Vardis as the alien cackled and coughed. He spat blood and looked at her. "You had your chance, Alex." Then he closed his eyes, never to open them again.

Alex was trying to get a grip on what had just happened.

She looked up at Team Boundless and the rest of the mech riders, watching to see what was going to happen.

Across from her, Roy had gotten to his feet and was approaching Alex. There was something off in his face. "You killed him," Roy murmured. "We were so close to destroying the Dark One, and you killed him."

Alex backed away, waving her hands. "No, Roy, it isn't what you think."

"You sold us out to the Dark One."

Roy's face was dark as he shook his head. "I'm sorry, Alex, but I can't let you leave."

Chine dropped from the sky and grabbed Alex in his claws. He took off into the air as Alex crawled up his arm and anchored herself to his back.

Chine swerved around some mech riders, heading for the open sky. *Vardis warped their memories. You saw the vision?*

Yeah, I saw it.

That's what they all believe to be true.

Alex's heart sank as she imagined Boundless believing she had betrayed them. *Everyone?*

Not everyone. I was able to shield Boundless, so they were only partially affected.

Alex thought it had been Chine who had protected her. *Wait, you didn't help me?*

No. That was not me.

Alex commed Boundless. "Team, on me! We need to get out of here."

No one answered at first, but then a steady stream of replies came in. Alex looked over her shoulder and saw Boundless peeling off from the rest of the riders surrounding the volcano. "Alex?" Jim asked. "What's going on?"

"I'll explain later. We need to get out of here now."

Boundless followed Alex as Roy walked over to Vardis' body. He knelt beside him and cradled Vardis' head. "You didn't deserve this, not after everything you did to help us." He closed the alien's eyes and commed the mech riders above. "Pursue Team Boundless."

The mech riders took off.

Roy stood in the volcano peered at Vardis, and his left eye started to twitch. It was the unease of a man who knew something was not right but did not understand what was amiss. He stared for some time at the alien's body.

CHAPTER TEN

Team Boundless didn't speak as they flew. Alex wasn't going to be the one to break the silence. Even she wasn't certain about what she'd just seen. She knew it wasn't true, much like the memories Vardis' had placed in her about her parents, yet they were there and as easy to recall as anything she'd experienced.

I couldn't have seen them since I was blind, she repeated to herself. She analyzed the vision from Vardis the same way, looking for the inconsistencies that only she could see and reminding herself of what she knew to be true while allowing Chine to fly unguided.

"We got bogies on our six!" Jim shouted.

Alex checked the area. The mech riders were closing in on Boundless. She had to get her head in the game. There was no way to know what the mech riders were planning to do to her and Boundless, but she wanted to be prepared for whatever came.

One of the mech riders opened a comm to Alex. "Team Boundless. We are ordering you to descend. You will be taken into custody. I repeat, descend."

Alex weighed her options. She knew the extent of Vardis' power, even during his dying breaths. Whatever was lodged in their minds was not going to be easily destroyed. "Negative," she replied.

As Alex was preparing to give orders to her team, the world went black around her, the back of her head erupting in pain.

It was the Dark One.

"Vardis' attack would have destroyed you if not for me," he said.

Alex burst out laughing. The Dark One had saved her? Why? "You're kidding. Why would you have saved *me*?" Alex asked.

"Consider it recompense. You saved my life. It was fitting that I saved yours."

Alex didn't know what to make of the statement. The Dark One being capable of something like honor went against everything she thought she knew about him.

Rather than engage with him, Alex concentrated on severing their connection. The darkness faded, and she was back with Team Boundless.

Gill and Brath were shouting, trying to find out what they were supposed to do.

Alex wracked her brain, attempting to come up with a plan to get them out of the mess they were in. "We're not going to fight them. Even if they don't know it, we're on the same team. Keep heading east. We'll lose them in the pixie forest. Their mechs can't keep up with us in the trees."

Jim's voice came through the comm. "How do you know that?"

Because this is the forest where we took out those giants on our date!

Alex didn't answer. Even if Boundless hadn't been affected by the illusion like the rest of the riders, it was obvious that there had been some disruption in their memories. "Do you guys trust me?"

The comm was silent.

Finally, Brath said, "Yeah. With my life."

Then Gill. "I'm with you."

Jollies, who had been shouting indiscernible words the whole time, finally managed, "Always, Alex."

There was silence again. Alex waited to hear what Jim said. "We're heading for the pixie forest, right? The one where we took out those giants?"

Alex breathed a sigh of relief. "Yeah, that one."

Jim slowed his mech down and fell behind the rest of Boundless. "Good. I got this one. I'll catch up with you guys later."

As the team sped past him, he let off ten proximity mines. Then he plunged into the forest beneath him.

The mech riders raced past where Jim had been, intent on dealing with Alex.

The mines went off as they flew over them, blinding the riders and disrupting their mechs.

Jim kicked in his thrusters to catch up with the rest of Boundless. They were flying through the forest, weaving between the trees while trying to stay as close to the ground as possible.

Alex pulled up her tactical map and surveyed the area. There was a cave up ahead, and earlier intel suggested it might be in use by the pixies of the area. "Jollies, I want you to go ahead and talk to the pixies. See if we can hole up in their cave. Got it?"

Jollies delivered an exceptionally chirpy "affirmative" and peeled off from the rest of the group.

Alex took Chine down to the ground and ordered the rest of Boundless to land.

The only dragon rider having a problem was Brath. Furi

was too large to move comfortably through the forest. "Brath, don't wait for us. You can't do this stealth stuff with Furi. Head to the coordinates I'm sending you and make sure it's safe."

Brath didn't bother responding, just took off toward the lake.

Alex turned to Gill and Jim, who had rejoined them. "We need to take this slow."

The three of them took their time moving through the forest, occasionally stopping to listen as the mech riders flew over them.

The forest was too dense for the mech riders to see through, and the trees covered any heat signatures Boundless might give off.

Gill watched the sky as Alex and Jim moved forward, occasionally calling out the position of the mech riders, who kept stopping and scanning for Boundless.

Jollies came rushing back, staying low. "The pixies say we can stay. We just have to get there fast."

The pixie cave wasn't far from the lake. Alex commed Brath, told him about the change of plans, and sent him the coordinates of the cave.

Under the setting sun, Boundless made their way to the cave, taking their time, ever aware of the riders above them. They made it to the cave without incident.

The pixies stood outside, watching Boundless anxiously. One of the pixies came forward and asked, "You two. You were here before, weren't you?"

Jim opened his mech and stuck his head out. "Yeah, we were. Weren't we?"

Alex leaped off Chine and approached the pixies. The tiny beings looked as if they were ready to flee, but they held their ground. "A little while ago," she said, "all of you escorted us on a date. Do you remember?"

The pixies flicked through different hues, eventually landing on a faded pink. "Yes, a date. It was truly awkward for you two. How could we forget? Come, come."

They led Boundless to their cave, which was much larger than a pixie cave had any reason to be. Boundless was easily able to fit inside, and their dragons rested on the outside, concealing themselves as best they could.

Alex and the rest of Boundless sat just inside, watching the mech riders flying overhead and waiting for the heat to die down.

Jim came over to Alex and took a seat beside her. "What's going on?"

Alex, who didn't take her eyes off the mech riders above, said, "We'll talk about it tomorrow. Is that cool?"

Jim nodded solemnly, and he and the rest of the team went farther into the pixie cave.

Alex continued to watch the mech riders long into the night. She didn't get to sleep until dawn approached.

Alex woke up the next morning under Chine's wings. She was nestled close to the dragon, his heartbeat making it difficult to join the land of the awake. *Ugh, Chine, I had the worst dream ever. Vardis tricked everyone into thinking I was a crappy person, and then we had to go on the run. It was the worst.*

Chine stood up and spread his wings, flapping them gently and sending dust everywhere. *Dustling, I am sorry to tell you that was not a dream.*

Alex stretched and got to her feet. *How long have I been out?*

Two days. The rest of Boundless went to the lake. They're waiting to hear from you.

Alex walked out from under Chine's wing and looked the

dragon in the eye. *I wish it had been a dream. Hey, you didn't keep me from Vardis' illusion, did you?*

Chine shook his head sadly. *No, I did not.*

It was the Dark One. He saved my life. I thought that was just a bad dream.

Chine scooped Alex into his claws as the pixies poured out of the cave. *Yes, he did. I don't know why he would do such a thing. He's safe from the shard now. Perhaps you two share a greater connection than you know.*

I don't want to think about that right now. I just want to see everyone. We can deal with it later.

Chine headed for the lake, not bothering to fly, informing Alex that they were keeping a lookout for the mech riders. They hadn't seen them for the last two days, but Gill and Jim weren't comfortable with the dragons being airborne yet.

It didn't take long to get to the lake, and they found the members of Team Boundless on the shore. The only person who had gone into the water was Brath. He was splashing around like a kid.

When Boundless saw Alex, they froze. Jollies was the first to move. She flew over and landed on her shoulder. The pixie hugged Alex tightly. "What's going on?"

Alex scratched the back of Jollies' neck, making the pixie giggle and shift to a bright red hue. "I don't know what you remember, but I know what I recall. Vardis was going to destroy our universe to kill the Dark One. I put a stop to it, but he's made it so no one else remembers that. I don't know what you think happened or how to make you believe me."

Jim just looked at Alex. "I remember that we came here on a date, and we talked about how much you wanted to stop the Dark One."

Gill was sitting on Timber. He lazily slid off and said, "We went to visit your family. They were amazing people. We had dinner, all of us and Vardis. Even then, none of us trusted him."

Jollies, who was still on Alex's shoulder, replied, "There was an explosion at the base. You were hurt, and then the comm went dead. We all thought it was Vardis."

Brath swam to the shore as Furi burst out of the water. He joined the rest of Boundless. "I remember you asking us if we trusted you. The answer is still yes."

Alex shook her head as she laughed. "What if I told you the Dark One saved my life? That he is the only reason I am still alive?"

The members of Boundless looked exchanged dubious glances. Finally, Brath stepped forward and extended his hand to Alex. "I would say I still trust you."

Alex wiped a tear away as she took Brath's hand and shook it.

"Why the hell are you smiling?" he asked.

Alex pulled him close and hugged him tightly. Slowly, the rest of Boundless came over and wrapped their arms around each other. "Because we saved the universe," she said. "Even if no one else knows it, we did it. All of us. We did this. Even if they think we're all traitors, we saved the entire universe, and we're not going to stop. Are you with me?"

No words had to be said. They held each other as their dragons surrounded them, covering Boundless with their wings.

Alex looked at the sky. It was clear, not a cloud in sight, just infinite blue.

Infinite possibilities.

THE END

Want to know what happens to Team Boundless? Love Middang3ard? Check out the other series set in Middang3ard: Dark Gate Angels. Team Boundless return in Dark Gate Angels to deliver a shocking twist. (Please note: the timeline of Dark Gate Angels is such that Alex's 'betrayal' happens in Dark Gate Angels, Book 2. Their epic return will be in Book 3.)

Join the battle against the Dark One today!

AUTHOR NOTES RAMY VANCE

JUNE 12, 2020

Click, Clack …

The day that I sat down to write these Author Notes is a special day for me. For this day is the day I have officially earned a full-time income off of my books for one full year.

A while back, I went to 20Book London and, pumped after the event, I decided I would wake up every morning at 5 am to write. When I told my wife that was my plan, she thought I was crazy.

And then on that first morning I woke up at 4:40 am and started banging away at my computer, my wife yelled two things from our bedroom:

One – I can't believe you're up.

And two – get the hell out of your office and go somewhere where I can't hear your damn keyboard click, clacking…

So, I moved out of my office to the much farther away kitchen table, where, for the next few months, I click, clacked every morning from 5 am until my son woke up at 7:27 am (and I'm not kidding … he wakes up at 7:27 on the dot almost every morning).

73

At that time, I wrote 6 days a week, no matter what.

And then I edited, worked on my marketing game, published, failed and tried again, until finally, little by little, I things started to improve.

I made plans. I stuck to them even when things looked wrong. I found mentors (Michael and Martha first among them) and listened to their advice even when I thought they were crazy (and believe you me ... Martha is certifiable).

But most importantly, I click, clacked every chance I got.

And it paid off. 1 year ago, I got that deposit from Amazon with a sum of money that equaled the magic number I needed to be full-time.

Yesterday I showed my wife how much writing has earned us over the last year. She was unimpressed. I'm not going to lie, that hurt and I called her on it.

Her response couldn't have been more perfect. "I'm not surprised. I always knew you'd get here. I always knew all that click, clacking will lead here."

(Sweet words, but despite them, I still write in the kitchen.)

AUTHOR NOTES MICHAEL ANDERLE

JUNE 14, 2020

So, I was click-clacking all over the lower part of the Las Vegas Strip in town early this year until I wasn't allowed to go anywhere.

Then, instead of writing "out there," I had to write and work in the office—an office that got kinda small, really. I'm happy we are opening up because I was going to go certifiable (it felt like.)

For me (this is back in Nov of 2015), my wife had no idea what I was doing with this writing stuff until one night, I was typing on my laptop as we were both in bed, and she finally looked over at me and asked. "I see you typing all the time. What are you doing?"

"Writing a book," I replied.

"Do what?" (It's not like I shared with her a compelling desire to write books my whole life, so this was news to her.)

"Writing a book. See, it's my third. I have two others already out for sale." I turned my laptop and showed her my little Amazon author page with those first two books.

I can't say she was too impressed (and since those were

the first covers I had for the Kurtherian Gambit series, I can't really blame her). However, she nodded in the right direction and let me go about my business.

That is all I needed from her at the time, and to this day, I appreciate that she asked, then let me go do it without asking too many questions I didn't have the answers for had she wanted them.

This happened when I was writing between books two and three. About six weeks later (after books 04 and 05 released, so call it mid-January), she asked me about income and sales and what I told her about my 2016 plans...

Didn't impress her much (again!)

I had BIG plans for 2016. When I shared my sales goals? *(Just an aside, she was responsible for over a hundred million dollars' worth of product lines for Alcon at the time)* Well, my goals...

Didn't cut the nine-figure mark (or even come close!)

So, I did what any self-respecting Texan would do. I shut up and stopped sharing what I was making with her.

Solved that problem nicely, don't you think?

Perhaps it didn't but I was having fun building a small publishing company and writing (clickity-clacking) my fingers to the bones to keep the stories coming, and I had replaced my normal income by this time. I didn't get rid of the other income, I had just doubled and then tripled it.

It's interesting how men are built. Like Ramy, I seek my wife's "attaguy," and she is the one who can lift my heart with the right words or a smile.

So, if your spouse is clickity-clacking away, just remember that at some point in their journey, they want to hear you say "attaboy" or "attagirl" and know that no matter how successful we authors become.

It's always the best when we know our loved ones have

our backs as we weave worlds with… perhaps…flying dragons in them.

Ad Aeternitatem,

Michael Anderle

OTHER BOOKS BY THE AUTHORS

Other Middang3ard Books

Never Split The Party (01)
Late To the Party (02)
It's My Party (03)
Blue Hell And Alien Fire (04)

Death Of An Author: A Middang3ard Novella

Dark Gate Angels

Other Books by Ramy Vance

Mortality Bites Series
Keep Evolving Series
Fatebound Series
Welcome to the Dragon Show Series

Other Books by Michael Anderle

CONNECT WITH THE AUTHORS

Connect with Ramy

Join Ramy's Newsletter to get a **FREE AUDIOBOOK!**
Join Ramy's FB Group: House of the GoneGod Damned!

Connect with Michael Anderle and sign up for his email list here:

Website: http://lmbpn.com

Email List: http://lmbpn.com/email/

Facebook:
www.facebook.com/TheKurtherianGambitBooks